THE MAN WHO RODE A TIGER
and other stories

Catherine Lim
illustrator Chen Tian-Ci

TARGET

Published by
the Paperback Division of
W.H. ALLEN & Co. PLC.

A Target Book
Published in 1985
by the Paperback Division of
W. H. Allen & Co. PLC
44 Hill Street, London W1X 8LB

First published in Singapore by Times Books
International, 1981

Printed in Great Britain by
Cox & Wyman Ltd, Reading

ISBN 0 426 20163 9

Contents

THE BRAHMIN
AND THE ROGUES

THERE WAS ONCE A Brahmin, Viravara by name, who was well known for his kindness to others and for his piety. He was always ready to share whatever he had with those who had less and he was so pious that he would pray for long hours and offer sacrifices to the gods whenever he could. He was by no means rich, and he worked hard to earn money to feed his family and to do charitable deeds among the people in his village.

Unfortunately, Viravara was a rather simple man and did not possess much intelligence. Indeed, some of the villagers thought him very stupid and were ready to take advantage of him. Instead of appreciating Viravara's kindness of heart, they saw him only as a stupid fellow who could provide them with fun and gain.

There was, however, one who saw the kindness and piety of Viravara and watched him closely to protect and help him. This was the goddess Chandika at whose shrine Viravara often prayed and offered sacrifices.

One day, Viravara decided to honour this goddess.

Her shrine was in the forest of Gotama, some distance from the village. Viravara decided to offer her a goat. He could not afford to get a big goat, but he had enough money for a small one.

Happily, Viravara counted his money and set out for a neighbouring village where he knew he could buy a goat. On the way, he met one of his neighbours, called Kitava, and told him about his plan.

"Ah, so you're on your way to get a goat!" exclaimed Kitava, his cunning eyes narrowing as a wicked plan formed in his head. "What a good man you are, Viravara!" he continued, smiling broadly. "But look here, it's a long way to the next village and to the forest of Gotama for your sacrifice. Why don't you come into my house and have a little cup of mango juice?"

Now it really was a hot day and Viravara was only too glad to accept Kitava's kind offer of mango juice.

He felt refreshed after the drink, and thanked Kitava profusely as he prepared to resume his walk to the village. "How kind the world is," thought Viravara with a glow in his heart as he left Kitava's house.

As soon as he had gone, Kitava rushed to see some of his friends. These friends were just as dishonest and cunning as Kitava. There was nothing they liked better than to play tricks on simple people like Viravara.

Kitava whispered his plan to them, and they nodded their heads eagerly, grinning at the thought of having fun at Viravara's expense. The rogues immediately got to work.

Viravara, having bought his goat from the village, carried it on his shoulders and began to make his way to the shrine of the goddess Chandika in the forest of

Gotama. On his way, he met one of the rogues who was casually leaning against a tree.

When Viravara came near, the rogue pretended to look startled. He stared at the goat which Viravara was carrying across his shoulders. "Why, Viravara, what are you doing with a dog on your shoulders?" he cried.

"A dog? What are you talking about?" replied Viravara. "It's a goat! I'm on my way to offer a sacrifice in the forest of Gotama!"

Viravara thought that the fellow was drunk. How could he mistake a goat for a dog? A dog was an unclean creature to a Brahmin. Imagine carrying a dog to offer to the goddess Chandika!

"I tell you it's a goat," said Viravara, as the fellow continued staring.

Finally, the rogue scratched his head, looked very puzzled and walked away.

A short while later, Viravara met the second rogue. He was casually plucking some leaves from a tree.

When Viravara came near, he stopped and pretended to look very surprised as he asked, "Where are you going, Viravara?"

"To offer this goat to the goddess Chandika in the forest of Gotama," said Viravara proudly.

"Goat, did you say goat?" asked the second rogue, opening his eyes very wide. "Why, that's a dog you're carrying on your shoulders!"

Viravara frowned. Now, here was another stupid fellow who could not tell a dog from a goat!

"Of course it's a goat!" cried Viravara. "You surely do not think I would offer an unclean creature like a dog to the goddess Chandika, do you?"

The rogue continued to stare at the goat. Then he

looked hard at Viravara as if he didn't understand what he had said. Finally, he shrugged his shoulders and walked away.

Viravara began to feel a little worried. "Something strange is happening this morning," he thought. "I wonder what it can be?"

He walked on and came upon the third rogue who was sitting under a tree, sharpening a stick. As soon as he saw Viravara, he started up as if in fright.

"Why, Viravara, where are you going?" he asked.

"To the forest of Gotama to offer the goddess Chandika this goat," replied Viravara.

"Why, Viravara, that's not a goat you're carrying, that's a dog!" cried the rogue. "How can you offer this unclean creature to the goddess?"

Viravara was really worried now. He thought, "I must have been cheated in the village. The goat-seller sold me a dog pretending that it was a goat. Three

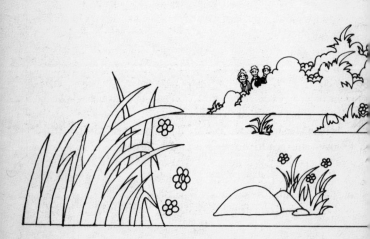

people have told me that it's a dog, not a goat! Oh, what a fool I've been!" He walked on, not knowing what to do.

Suddenly he saw Kitava. With him was a dog which had a rope tied round its neck.

"Viravara, why are you carrying a dog on your shoulders?" cried Kitava, pretending to look astonished. "I thought you were going to buy a goat to offer to the goddess Chandika?"

"Am I not carrying a goat?" cried poor Viravara, ready to burst into tears.

"Oh, my poor man, can't you tell the difference between a dog and a goat?" exclaimed the cunning Kitava. Then he pretended to look as if he understood everything. "Ah, Viravara, I know, I know!" he cried. "It must be the effect of the mango drink I gave you this morning. The juice obviously does not agree with you. It's causing you to see things wrongly as if you were drunk!"

"That's it!" cried Viravara. "I shouldn't have taken the drink. It has clouded my mind and made me do a silly thing! Oh, what shall I do now? I must get rid of this dog, and I don't have enough money to buy a goat for the sacrifice!" Poor Viravara was crestfallen.

"Ah, my good friend, let me help you," said the sly Kitava. "This is all my fault, for I gave you the mango drink. Look, let me give you this goat of mine," he continued, showing Viravara the dog beside him. "You see what a big, beautiful goat it is? You may have it for your sacrifice."

Viravara looked at the animal and puzzled. Oh dear! The mango drink was indeed affecting him very badly! He was confusing dogs with goats. He had better accept Kitava's kind offer quickly and make his offerings to the goddess Chandika before anything else happened.

"In exchange for this goat, let me have your dog," said Kitava. "I see that it's a huge, fierce-looking creature which will do very nicely for a watchdog."

So Kitava handed over his goat to Viravara and took the dog and hoisted it on his shoulders.

The three rogues were watching all this from their hiding places behind some trees and bushes. Barely able to contain their mirth, they were eagerly looking forward to a feast of mutton curry that Kitava's wife would make from Viravara's goat.

Now, unknown to all, the goddess Chandika was watching all this. She was very angry with the four evil men for having played such a nasty trick on simple Viravara. "Let's see who will laugh at the end," she said.

She made a few signs and, lo and behold! The goat that Kitava had taken from Viravara turned into a huge, ugly, fierce dog that snarled so ferociously at the rogues that they ran away, screaming in terror. As for the dog on Viravara's shoulders, it turned into the handsomest and healthiest goat that had ever been offered in sacrifice. Pleased with Viravara's piety and devotion, the goddess Chandika granted him many blessings. He became prosperous and happy and remained so for the rest of his days.

THE BOASTFUL WIFE

KAMALA WAS VERY HAPPY. She smiled and laughed and talked excitedly to everyone she met. You see, Kamala's husband Shankar, who worked as a gardener in the royal gardens of the Raja, had just been promoted to Chief Gardener.

He deserved the promotion because he was a hardworking and conscientious worker. He worked all day, never minding the hot sun and the backaches. He kept the Raja's lawns green and lush. The flower beds were always full of bright flowers of every imaginable hue, and free from weeds. The bushes were always well trimmed. No tree or plant ever died from lack of water or nourishment. It was no wonder then that the Raja was pleased with Shankar and made him Chief Gardener!

Kamala boasted loudly of her husband's skill as a gardener to all the people in the village. She loved to talk about any pleasant thing that happened to herself or to her husband. She told her friends happily that her husband would now be able to get her a new nose-ring.

"Oooh! Aaah!" exclaimed the women in envy and

Kamala was very pleased. She loved to hear the "ooohs" and "aaahs" of admiration and envy from her friends. Meanwhile, Shankar worked harder than ever.

One hot night, he just could not fall asleep, so he decided to take a stroll in the lovely, moonlit royal gardens. He tiptoed out of the house for fear of waking his wife. As Shankar walked towards the gardens, he suddenly stopped. He stared — he could not believe his eyes! There, some distance from him in the moonlight, was a white elephant nibbling at the fresh green grass on the lawn.

Shankar's mind was in a whirl. A white elephant, white as snow! He suddenly remembered the story of Indra and Airavata, a story related to him long ago by his mother. Indra was the King of the Gods in Heaven and Airavata was the beautiful, snow-white elephant he rode from one place to another.

"This must be Airavata!" thought Shankar with mounting excitement. "So Airavata has come down from Heaven and is visiting Earth! It must be getting tired of the food it gets in Heaven! See how eagerly it's eating the grass here!"

The white elephant went on nibbling quietly.

Then Shankar had an idea. "Airavata will be returning to Heaven after its feed," he thought. "If I catch hold of its tail before it flies off, I too will be able to go up with it. Then I shall be able to see all the wonderful things in Heaven!"

He moved up quietly, hid behind a tree and waited patiently for Airavata to finish eating. The elephant ate and ate, but just as dawn was breaking, it finished its meal and prepared to return home. Shankar knew this was the moment. He ran up and caught hold of the elephant's tail. Airavata rose into the air, as light as a bird, and Shankar rose with it.

Soon, they were flying high above the clouds. When they reached Heaven, Shankar stared at the many beautiful things that met his eyes. Vast stretches of greenery, with rows and rows of trees laden with ripe fruit! There were flowers with colours that Shankar had never seen before, giving off perfumes that he had never smelt before. Everywhere he looked, he saw things that made him open his eyes wide in admiration and disbelief.

The trees, plants and flowers were ten times as big as those on Earth, ten times as fresh and ten times as bright. The fruits also looked ten times juicier and tastier. Oh, how Shankar marvelled!

When dusk came, Shankar remembered that he had to return to Earth. Airavata was getting ready for its nightly visit to the Raja's royal gardens. Shankar thought, "Kamala is sure to scold me for being away so long, but I shall take back a present for her from Heaven. That will keep her quiet."

He chose an areca nut which was as big as a coconut. Kamala loved to chew the areca nut, so that would make her happy and she would forget to scold him. Then, holding on to Airavata's tail, Shankar returned to Earth. He quickly went home to his wife.

"Just where have you been all this time?" she demanded angrily, her hands on her hips.

"Heaven," replied Shankar promptly. Then he showed her the giant areca nut.

Imagine Kamala's surprise. She had never seen an areca nut this big. Then a smile stole over her face. What a lot to boast about to her friends. An areca nut as large as a coconut, from Heaven!

19

She was getting ready to leave the house in a hurry with the marvellous news when Shankar stopped her.

"This is a very big secret indeed," he warned. "You mustn't tell everyone for Airavata may not come here again if you do."

"Oh, all right," said Kamala, but she was bursting to boast about it. What? Such a marvellous thing to talk about and she was to keep her mouth shut! It was the most difficult thing in her life, but she managed to keep the secret. She wanted to see what other wonderful things her husband would bring back from Heaven.

On his next trip, Shankar brought a mango that was as large as a pumpkin. It was the juiciest, most delicious mango that Kamala had ever tasted in her life. How she longed to run to her neighbours and tell them about the areca nut and the mango and to hear their "ooohs" and "aaahs". Still she managed to keep the secret.

However, during the next visit, Shankar brought back a giant rose which gave out the loveliest perfume. Kamala could not restrain herself any longer. When her neighbour, Lakshmi, commented, "My, what a lovely perfume you're using," Kamala cried out, "It's not perfume, it's the scent of a giant rose from Heaven!" Then she went on excitedly, telling Lakshmi about Airavata's visits, the areca nut and the mango.

Lakshmi's eyes opened wide in wonder. She quickly ran to tell her friend, who told *her* friend, who told her neighbour, who told her in-laws, until very soon the whole village knew about the visits of the heavenly elephant, Airavata, and the marvellous things that Shankar the Chief Gardener had been bringing back from his trips to Heaven. They all whispered in great excitement. All wanted to see the beautiful, snow-white elephant and all secretly longed to follow Shankar to Heaven to see the wonderful things there.

So, the next evening, all the villagers came to Shankar's house, begging to be allowed to go with him to Heaven. Kamala, who felt very important, demanded that her husband take all of them.

Poor Shankar was dismayed, but there was nothing that he could do. He agreed reluctantly.

That night, all of them trooped to the Raja's gardens and waited behind trees and bushes for Airavata to come down. When it came down at last, so white and beautiful it was that the villagers gasped in wonder.

"There, I told you!" whispered Kamala triumphantly, enjoying herself greatly.

The elephant, as usual, began eating grass. At dawn, it prepared to take off on its flight back to Heaven. Shankar beckoned to the rest to go up quietly. He himself ran up and grasped the elephant's tail. Kamala held on to his feet, Lakshmi held Kamala's feet and Lakshmi's husband held on to her feet. Their neighbours held on to his feet, their neighbour's mother-in-law held on to their feet and so on. When Airavata rose into the air, therefore, a long chain of men and women trailed after him, led by Shankar.

"Oh, this is exciting!" cried Kamala. "I told you so, didn't I? Isn't it wonderful that because of my husband and me, all of you are now making a trip to Heaven?"

She went on to boast about the beautiful things that Shankar had told her he had seen. She described them as if she herself had been there before. She even told them the sizes of the vegetables and fruits and flowers.

"I'm particularly keen to bring back a melon," cried Lakshmi. "Now, Kamala, tell me again, how big is it?"

Now Kamala did not know how big the heavenly melon was, but she said, "Very big indeed. It would be enough to feed you and your family for a week, at least!"

"Yes, but exactly how big is that?" insisted Lakshmi.

"Shankar, how big exactly is the melon from Heaven?" Kamala asked her husband.

To prevent any more questioning, Shankar decided to demonstrate the size by stretching out both arms. As he did this, he let go of Airavata's tail, and so the whole chain of men and women came tumbling down to earth!

Shankar fell on top of Kamala who fell on top of Lakshmi who fell on top of her mother-in-law, and so on, until there was a huge heap of men and women on the lawn of the Raja's garden.

As you can guess, Airavata never came to the Raja's garden again.

THE FAITHFUL PRINCE

A VERY, VERY LONG TIME AGO, in a city in northern India, there lived a king who had seven sons. They grew into fine, handsome young men. When they reached a marriageable age, their father called the Prime Minister to him and said, "I want you to find seven brides for my seven sons. They must be beautiful and virtuous women, for my sons deserve no less!"

The Prime Minister always consulted a fortune-teller, the most famous in the land, whenever he had any difficult task to perform. This was the most difficult job he had been given so far, he thought, and so he went in haste to the fortune-teller.

He was a wise old man with a long, white beard. The fortune-teller told him that the best way for the seven Princes to get wives they wanted was this: they were to go to the grazing grounds outside the city on an appointed day and shoot arrows in the direction of the city. The girl who lived in the house nearest to where an arrow fell would marry the Prince who shot it.

The Prime Minister gave the King the fortune-teller's advice. After giving the matter some very careful thought, the King decided to do as he was told for the fortune-teller was known far and wide for his wisdom.

On the day appointed by the fortune-teller, the seven Princes assembled in the grounds outside the city, ready with their gleaming arrows. A large crowd had gathered to watch the exciting event. Of course, all the eligible girls in the city stayed indoors, each hoping that an arrow would fall near her house.

Now although all the Princes were handsome, fine young men, the one who was considered the most handsome was the youngest. His name was Rudra. Each girl secretly hoped to become his bride.

At the given sign, the seven Princes shot their arrows and a murmur of excitement ran through the crowd as the seven golden arrows, gleaming in the sunshine, flew through the air. Then seven servants were sent to look for the arrows and bring back the seven brides.

One, two, three, four, five, six beautiful young girls, blushing like roses, were brought before the Princes. But where was the seventh arrow?

A thorough search was conducted but the seventh arrow — that from the bow of Prince Rudra — just could not be found. Everyone was puzzled.

Then, someone happened to look upwards. There, sitting on a branch of a very tall tree, was an ugly monkey holding the arrow! Imagine the astonishment, then the horror of the crowd. What! Was the handsome Prince Rudra to have a monkey for his bride?

The Prime Minister, who was filled with alarm, suggested that the Prince be given another arrow to

shoot. Everyone agreed that this was the best thing to do. But Prince Rudra shook his head slowly. There was a very serious look on his face. "No, no," he said. "I took an oath and I cannot break it. The monkey has my arrow, and is therefore my bride."

The King and the Prime Minister, the six Princes and all the people present protested, then pleaded. But Prince Rudra was firm.

"I cannot break a solemn promise," he repeated. He gently led the monkey down from the tree and took her home.

Preparation for the weddings of the six Princes went ahead. Six big, beautiful houses were built and gardens and orchards laid out as the King's wedding gifts to six of his sons. But for Prince Rudra, there was nothing. Everyone was ashamed to look upon him and the monkey he had claimed for his bride.

Prince Rudra took the monkey to a modest house on the outskirts of the city and settled there. He spent his time quietly, planting vegetables and flowers. He took good care of the monkey, feeding her well and sometimes taking her for walks along the river bank. She was a quiet, docile creature, never giving any trouble and learning to please the Prince by doing his bidding.

The King, meanwhile, was still fretting about the strange turn of events. He thought hard on how to make Prince Rudra give up the monkey.

Once more, he consulted the Prime Minister who soon came up with an idea.

"Your Majesty," he said, "go to each of your sons and tell them you are going to dine at his house. Each of their wives must prepare a banquet worthy of Your Majesty. Those who are able to please Your Majesty will be rewarded with jewels, but the one who is unable to prepare any food will be cast off as unworthy!"

The Prime Minister, by this plan, hoped that the monkey would be cast off, since she would not be able to prepare a feast.

The King was pleased with the idea. He sent word to all his seven sons that he was going to visit them, beginning with the eldest. The wives of the six Princes were delighted for they knew they could prepare the most tasty dishes for the King.

Prince Rudra, however, was dismayed. He looked pityingly at the monkey and said, "You poor thing. Everyone wants to get rid of you. But I shall always be faithful to you for I chose you."

Suddenly, to his amazement, the monkey began to speak. "Have no fear. Take this earthen jar and break it against the tree where you found me. There, you will be told what to do. Your father will have the most magnificent banquet he has ever seen!"

Full of astonishment, Prince Rudra followed the monkey's instructions. He took the earthen jar which the monkey gave him and hurried to the place where the tree stood, tall and majestic. There, he broke the jar against the trunk.

As the pieces fell to the ground, he heard a strange cracking sound, as that of wood being torn apart. He looked up and saw that the trunk of the tree had opened to reveal a beautiful nymph. She was so beautiful that Prince Rudra could hardly take his eyes off her.

"Ah, Prince Rudra," she said, in a voice that was sweetly melodious, "I am the Nymph of this tree, and I have been in love with you for a long time. I would like to be your bride."

"But that's impossible!" gasped Prince Rudra. "I have a bride already and I love her!"

"What! An ugly, hairy monkey?" remarked the Nymph scornfully. "How can you, a handsome Prince, throw yourself away on such a miserable creature? Cast her off at once!"

"No, I'll never do that!" cried Prince Rudra with determination. "I vowed to protect her and I always will!"

"Ah, there's no need for you to protect her anymore, for I've killed her!" cried the Nymph.

"What!" exclaimed the Prince in fright. "Surely you have done no such thing?"

"See for yourself then," said the Nymph. As she spoke, she pointed upwards to the topmost branches of the tree. There, hanging over a branch, was a piece of the monkey's skin!

When Prince Rudra saw this, he cried out in his shock and grief. Then, leaning against the tree, he wept.

He felt a gentle tap on his shoulder.

"Grieve no more, Prince Rudra, for look, I am she!" cried the Nymph.

When Prince Rudra lifted his head to look, he saw the Nymph in the process of transforming herself into a monkey. Then, before the Prince could get over his astonishment, the monkey had transformed herself into the beautiful Nymph again!

"My wonderful Prince," cried the Nymph, her face radiant with joy. "I searched all over the earth among mankind for a husband and I fell in love with you. But I had to test your love first, for many men are fickle and untrue. So I took on the shape of a monkey and

caught your arrow as it flew over the tree. The rest you know. I am your wife, if you will have me."

With these words, the Nymph knelt before the Prince. Imagine his amazement. One surprise after another! But how wonderful it had all turned out to be!

The Prince led his bride back to his house. The next morning, he awoke and found that instead of his humble house, there stood a splendid, gleaming palace surrounded by lush gardens and orchards! The trees in the orchards were laden with the most beautiful fruits the Prince had ever seen.

"Your father, the King, will be coming on a visit soon," said the Nymph. "Everything will be to his satisfaction."

When the King came, accompanied by the Prime Minister, the six Princes and their wives, they were all dazed by the splendour around them. Never before had they seen such a beautiful palace, such rich furnishings and such luxuriant gardens! They could only gape and wonder. And the food that was laid before them! One hundred dishes of delicious meats, vegetables and fruits and goblets of rare wine such that they had never tasted before.

Their greatest surprise was when the bride was presented to them. In place of the ugly, hairy monkey stood a woman whose beauty dazzled them all!

The King was so pleased that he showered upon her the costliest jewels. But, more than any costly jewel, the Nymph valued the love of her faithful Prince.

THE MAN WHO
RODE A TIGER

ONE COLD AND RAINY NIGHT, Tiger came out of the forest soaking wet. There was a hut near by, and Tiger decided to wait under its thatched eaves for the rain to stop. Inside the hut lived an old woman who liked to talk to herself as old women often do. She was moving about busily inside with her pots and pans trying to catch the rain water leaking through her roof.

As she placed this pot here and that pan there, she grumbled aloud, "Drip, drip, drip, drip! Drip all the time! This perpetual dripping gives no rest to a poor old woman."

Tiger, who was listening intently, began to wonder who or what this Perpetual Dripping was. It was said to be "terrible" by the old woman, and it was always after her, giving her no rest. Tiger listened again, quite interested in finding out more about Perpetual Dripping.

"I'm sick and tired!" exclaimed the old woman. "This perpetual dripping will be the death of me!"

Tiger stiffened in fright. That Perpetual Dripping, whatever it was, would soon kill the poor old woman.

Tiger began to think that it must be a giant or a powerful monster or an evil spirit. Whatever it was, Tiger had no wish to meet it.

Tiger shivered in the darkness. Was Perpetual Dripping somewhere around now? Would he attack poor, harmless Tiger? Tiger began to wish that he had never come out of the forest. He would have been much safer there.

Suddenly in the darkness, Tiger heard a rough voice and he began to tremble with fear. This must be Perpetual Dripping, he thought.

"Come along," said a man's voice. "Let's get home now."

Actually, it was Bakoo the potter. He was a little drunk, having taken more wine than was good for him. He had left his donkey tethered near one of the huts, and now in the darkness he had mistaken Tiger for his donkey!

Of course, Tiger did not know this. He was so frightened that he did not dare do anything. He stood very still, hoping this dreadful Perpetual Dripping would not harm him.

Bakoo grasped Tiger and got up on his back. "Let's go," he said drunkenly, and he rode Tiger all the way to his home which was in the next village. Back home, he tied Tiger to a post near his hut and went to sleep. He slept very soundly indeed.

The next morning there was a great commotion in Bakoo's house. His wife rushed into the bedroom and, shaking her husband hard, asked him excitedly, "How did you come home last night?"

"Why, I rode home," said Bakoo sleepily.

"What! Can't you see the beast tethered outside?"

Bakoo's wife ran outside where a lot of people had

gathered at a safe distance from Tiger. She cried out to everyone, "Bakoo rode home on this tiger last night! Can you imagine anything braver than that?"

There was a great buzz of excitement as everyone began talking at once, praising Bakoo and exclaiming over Tiger.

"What a brave man!"

"Nobody has ever ridden a tiger before!"

"What a huge, ferocious beast!"

"The King must know of this!"

"Yes, yes, we must tell the King at once!"

In their excitement, they ran off in all directions to spread the news.

When Bakoo came out of the hut a while later and saw Tiger, he just could not believe what he had done and fainted straight away.

News of the brave thing he had done quickly spread through the country and indeed had already reached the King's ears. The King was most excited when told of Bakoo's deed which the people were only too eager to describe.

"He was not afraid at all. I saw with my own eyes how he tamed the tiger!"

"The tiger was a most ferocious beast with very long, sharp teeth, but Bakoo showed not the least bit of fear."

"Each time the tiger refused to go on, Bakoo dug into its side with his foot."

"At one point, the tiger nearly threw Bakoo off its back but he was so strong that he managed to stay on."

So the stories increased both in length and colour and Bakoo's reputation as the bravest man in the country was quickly established.

The King wished to see for himself if Bakoo could ride a tiger. He said, "I have a most ferocious wild tiger in my palace grounds. It is very huge. I would like to see Bakoo ride it!"

Poor Bakoo! When he heard of the King's wish, he turned pale with terror. How was he going to ride this fierce, powerful tiger? He had never even ridden a horse in his life! The only animal he was used to was the donkey.

Bakoo's wife said, "Never mind, husband, our sister-in-law's uncle has a horse. I will borrow it for you to practise riding on. It's a fierce horse and will give you good practice before you ride the King's tiger!"

40

Bakoo was so nervous that he would have liked to have run away, but his wife was firm. She borrowed the horse and made Bakoo mount it.

"But I can't, I'll fall off," stammered poor Bakoo.

"Nonsense, you won't. I'll tie you to the horse with ropes," said his wife.

So she brought along a coil of strong rope and tied Bakoo on to the back of the horse, leaving his arms and legs free. The horse became impatient with all the fuss and began to gallop off. Bakoo was thrown into panic. He began to shout for help. His shouts frightened the horse and made it go faster. Bakoo

waved his arms about wildly, trying to catch hold of anything he could to save himself. He caught hold of a branch of a small tree and the speed at which the horse was running caused the whole tree to be uprooted. Bakoo held on to the tree, terrified and yelling all the time. Fortunately for him, one of the small branches of the tree caught the horse in the eye and it fell down with an enormous thud.

Bakoo's wife's sister-in-law's uncle, who was the owner of the horse, came up angrily to scold Bakoo for injuring his horse. Soon a large crowd of people gathered. They stared open-mouthed at Bakoo holding an uprooted tree in his hand and sitting on top of a fallen horse. Some of the people ran to the King to tell him the exciting news.

"Bakoo rode a fierce, wild horse this time, but he was too strong for the horse."

"The poor creature was badly injured."

"Moreover, Bakoo pulled up a tree with his bare hands while on horseback."

"A big, enormous tree!"

"What a powerful man!"

"The bravest man in the world!"

On hearing this, the King was no longer keen to see Bakoo ride his tiger in case he injured it as he had injured the horse. After all, it was a rare and precious tiger and the King's favourite beast.

So the King sent for Bakoo and said, "I am sorry but I have now changed my mind about you riding my tiger. My tiger is at present recovering from a chill, and I don't want it to be taxed in any way. However, I have heard all about your brave deeds, and one of these days you must come to my palace to perform for me. I know of a wrestler who has the strength of two elephants, and I would like you to wrestle with him. There is a huge cobra whose mouth opens as wide as a cave. I would like to see you fight with it. And I have also heard of a crocodile that has eaten fifty men."

Poor Bakoo was so frightened that he nearly fainted. That night, while everyone was sleeping, Bakoo stole away from his village, riding his donkey, and he was never heard of again.

THE UNGRATEFUL ONE

A LONG TIME AGO, in a place called Bangalore in India, there lived a Brahmin. He was a simple and holy man who spent much of his time praying. He would sit very still, like a statue, close his eyes tightly and pray for hours.

Now, the Brahmin's wife was not too pleased about this for the Brahmin was so busy praying and doing kind deeds for people that he was always neglecting his own family. Indeed, they were very poor and often went to bed hungry.

"My good man," said the Brahmin's wife rather sharply to her husband one day. "Look into our rice pot. It is empty. Look at your three little sons. Their stomachs are flat from hunger! Aren't you going to do anything at all about this!"

On hearing his wife's angry words, the Brahmin suddenly realised that he had not been doing his duty to his family. He felt rather ashamed of himself. "I must see what I can do for my poor wife and children," he thought.

He walked out of their little bare house with no idea of where he was going. He just walked on and on in the light morning sunshine. Soon, he reached a dense forest. It was a dark, gloomy forest and the trees rose tall and silently around him.

The Brahmin sat down on a rock to rest and began to fan himself. Suddenly he paused . . . he thought he heard faint cries for help. They were coming from somewhere near him. He looked around. No man or beast was in sight. Where were the cries coming from?

The Brahmin suddenly realised that they were coming from the ground a short distance away from him. How odd! he got up and went closer to the source of the sounds. Yes, they were definitely coming from beneath the earth. There was a dense growth of bushes and creepers there. The Brahmin carefully parted these, and found, to his amazement, that he was looking down into a very deep pit.

At the bottom of the pit were a man, a tiger and a snake. They had obviously fallen into the pit which was really a trap. They were all looking up at the Brahmin and crying plaintively.

"Please help me, kind Brahmin!" the tiger said. "Dear Brahmin, I have a family waiting for me at home. I must get back to them! Please help me get out!"

The Brahmin replied, "Now, now, tiger, how can I be sure that you will not eat me if I rescue you?"

The tiger cried, "I give you my word of honour, Brahmin. I may look ferocious but I have harmed no one. Please get me out of this pit!"

The Brahmin felt sorry for the tiger and so he helped him out.

"Thank you so much, dear Brahmin," said the tiger. "Now, far from eating you, I would like to show my gratitude! I live in a cave in that high mountain

48

peak over there. Should you ever need help, please come to me, and I shall give you more than what you ask for! Now goodbye and thank you again!" The tiger bounded off.

"Brahmin, Brahmin, what about me?" cried the snake from the bottom of the pit.

"Oh no! I see you are black and you are poisonous and deadly!" cried the Brahmin in fear.

"Dear Brahmin, it is not my fault that I am made this way," pleaded the snake. "Rescue me, and I promise I will reward you richly too!"

The Brahmin felt sorry for the snake and decided to help it out. The snake was full of gratitude when it was at last out of the pit.

"Don't forget," it said, before gliding away, "to call me any time you need help. I will not disappoint you!"

Now there was only the man left in the pit.

"Surely you are not going to leave me here, Brahmin!" he cried rather impatiently. "Since you have shown kindness to animals, you will surely not neglect a fellow human being. Listen, I am Somnath, the famous goldsmith of Bangalore. I promise you that if you rescue me, I shall sell you gold or buy gold from you at very advantageous terms to you."

The Brahmin, hearing this, chuckled to himself. He thought, "How can a poor man like me ever think of buying or selling gold?" However, he quickly helped Somnath the goldsmith out of the pit.

"Thank you, I must now hurry back to my premises," cried Somnath and he ran off.

Some days later, the Brahmin looked at his hungry wife and children and said, "I must go to the tiger, the snake and the goldsmith for help. If they would only give me money to buy food, how happy I should be."

So the Brahmin went to the tiger's home which was a cave in the highest mountain peak near the forest. The tiger was very pleased to see him.

"Dear Brahmin, I've been waiting for you to come. I've got something for you!" cried the tiger excitedly.

The Brahmin could not believe his eyes when he saw what the tiger had. It was a heap of glittering jewels — gold necklaces and bracelets, ruby rings and earrings!

"Where did you get these?" cried the Brahmin in astonishment.

The tiger explained. "Well, it was like this. A wealthy nobleman, grandly dressed and wearing rich jewels, was out hunting in the forest. He was clearly determined to put an arrow through my heart. But I caught him first. I pounced on him and he, in his terror, begged me to take all the jewels he was wearing and let him go. They looked very costly, and I thought of you and of how much you would like them. So I agreed to the bargain!"

The Brahmin had never seen such rich glittering jewels. "I know what I'll do," he said. "I'll take them to Somnath the goldsmith and see how much they are worth!"

Now when Somnath saw the gold and ruby ornaments that the Brahmin brought to him, his eyes opened wide in astonishment. He recognised the jewels as those which had belonged to the King's son. The Prince often went about dressed in his grand clothes and wearing his jewels. He wore these jewels even when he went hunting which was much against the wishes of his father.

Somnath did not tell the Brahmin what he knew. A crafty plot was hatching in his head. He did not want the Brahmin to possess such wealth; he wanted a share of it himself. He told the Brahmin to wait while he sent to get the money to pay him for the jewels. However, instead of getting the money, he went to the King and told him that the Brahmin had waylaid the Prince in the forest and robbed him of his jewels. He hoped the King would give him some of the jewels as a reward.

When the King heard Somnath's story, he was angry and sent his soldiers to get the Brahmin. The poor Brahmin was thrown into prison. Somnath smiled an evil smile.

The poor Brahmin was full of misery as he sat in his prison cell. "Who can help me now?" he moaned. Suddenly, he thought of the snake. His eyes lit up. "Snake," he called urgently. "Come to me, I need your help."

To his amazement, the snake was beside him in a moment.

"Oh, how glad I am to see you, snake," wept the Brahmin and he told the snake the whole story of how he came to be in prison.

"I know what I shall do," cried the snake. "I shall go into the King's chamber tonight and bite him. His servants, seeing me, will know how deadly my poison is. They will be in a state of panic. I will spread the word that only you, the Brahmin, can save the King. You will go up to him and touch him three times on his head. The poison will then go away and have no effect. Then you will tell the whole story to the King and he will believe you!"

So the snake carried out its plan. While the King was sleeping, it bit him on the leg. The King's screams brought his servants running to him. They were just in

time to see the snake gliding out of the chamber.

"A black snake with a flat head!" they gasped in fear. The King began to moan and writhe in pain, but

his doctors could do nothing.

"Oh, I shall die," groaned the King.

Then word came to the King's ears that only the holy Brahmin whom he had thrown into prison could cure him.

"Send for him immediately," groaned the King.

The Brahmin was brought into the King's chambers. He touched the King's forehead three times with his fingers. To the amazement of all, the King immediately sat upright on his bed. He was no longer in pain — the poison was gone!

Seizing this opportunity, the Brahmin began to give the true account of how he had obtained the Prince's jewels.

When he had finished, the King said, "Forgive me, dear Brahmin, for treating you so unjustly. You shall have all the jewels, together with a house and a plot of land as compensation for this unfair treatment."

Then, raising his voice in anger, the King ordered his soldiers to get the evil Somnath and throw him into prison. The Brahmin and his family no longer went hungry. Indeed, they remained happy and prosperous till the end of their lives.

NOT TIME YET

IN THE GREAT AND beautiful city of Vikram-apura lived a king named Lakshadatta. We will call him King Lak for short. This king was well-known for his generosity towards his followers and attendants. He would reward those who served him well with rich gifts of jewels, fine clothes and horses. Himself blessed with good fortune, he was ready to share it with others. Indeed, the name Lakshadatta meant "Giver of Riches".

One of the attendants of King Lak was a man named Labhadatta. Let us call *him* Lab. He was always dressed only in a tattered piece of animal skin used as a loincloth. His ribs showed through his skin, his cheeks were sunken, his hair was always matted. Everything pointed to his poverty. Yet, he was uncomplaining and served the King well.

Now why didn't King Lak, the Giver of Riches, help poor Lab? Well, Lab was poor by choice. He had once been very rich and famous but had led an evil life. Great misfortune then fell on him. He lost all his wealth and was struck down by sickness. A holy man told him that this was the punishment for the evil life he had led.

Hearing this, Lab felt great sorrow for his sins. When he recovered from his illness, he decided to make atonement by giving up his wicked ways and leading the life of a poor beggar. He wandered around for some time, dressed only in his loincloth and allowing his hair to grow long.

"When I have paid for all my sins," Lab said, "fortune will come my way again. Meanwhile, I shall be content to be poor and humble."

So it was that he wandered into the city of Vikramapura where he became one of King Lak's attendants.

The King knew the story of Lab's life. This was why he did not want to reward the man with the generous gifts he always bestowed upon those who served him well. Since Lab's poverty was a means of making atonement for his sinful life, to give him riches now might only prevent him from making full atonement.

"When he has fully paid for his sins, I shall reward him, but not before then," thought wise King Lak.

"When the Giver of Riches rewards me, I shall know my period of penitence is over," thought the humble Lab.

So he continued to serve King Lak while the other followers and attendants wondered why the Giver of Riches did not give anything to this faithful and loyal servant.

One day, the King, who was very fond of hunting, went to a forest which was well known for its variety of wild animals. He was seated on an elephant and carried a bow. A ferocious tiger suddenly appeared. Without any warning, it rushed at the elephant. The beast took fright and, in its terror, threw the King from his seat to the ground! Imagine the alarm of the attendants! At that very moment, a wild boar suddenly appeared and made to rush upon the King who was still lying on the ground. Without a moment's hesitation, Lab dashed forward. Armed with only a pole, he hit the creature again and again until it fell, stunned, to the ground.

All marvelled at Lab's bravery. They wondered that this thin starved man could get the better of a boar.

The King longed to reward him with riches from the royal treasure chamber, but remembered that Lab was still paying for his sins. He became impatient for the time when the period of atonement would be over.

"How I long to shower wealth upon this man!" he thought. "But I must not interfere with the ways of Fortune. Only when it is time for Fortune to come to Lab again will I give him riches."

The King's impatience, however, continued. "I know what to do," thought the generous man with a sudden light in his eyes. "I have a plan by which I can see if it is time for the good Lab to enjoy fortune again!"

He went into his garden where all kinds of fruit trees grew. The King was particularly fond of the citron fruit. He plucked the finest looking citron from one of the trees and took it to his chamber of riches. There, selecting the finest jewels, he cleverly stuffed them into the citron.

That evening, sitting in his royal chair, with his attendants around him, he called for Lab to come before him. "I would like to give you a reward," said the King.

Lab came forward eagerly.

King Lak brought out the citron. "Here you are," he said, giving the citron to Lab.

Lab took it humbly but in his heart he thought, "What's this? A citron? Then it is not time for me to enjoy good fortune yet!"

The other attendants who were looking on also wondered. "A citron? How can the King reward brave

Lab who saved his life with only a citron?"

Coming out of the palace into the streets, Lab met a wandering beggar who looked at the rich, ripe fruit with longing. Felling sorry for him, Lab gave him the fruit and walked away.

Now the beggar remembered that the citron was the favourite fruit of King Lak so, hoping to get a rich reward, he hastened into the palace and offered the King the fruit.

"Why, who gave you this citron?" asked the King.

When he was told that it was Lab, he knew it was not time yet for the man to enjoy good fortune — his sins had not been fully atoned yet.

Some time later, the King again sent for Lab. When the man appeared before him, the King again brought out a citron. This too had been stuffed with jewels, but of course nobody knew this. "Here's a gift for you," said the King, handing the citron to Lab.

Lab took it humbly and again wondered, "The King must think I like citrons very much! I shall take it. It's not time yet for me to have great riches."

As he was leaving the palace, he met one of the palace servants who commented that he had never ever seen such a beautiful fruit. He offered Lab some money for it. Lab accepted the offer eagerly, for he was hungry and the money would buy him a square meal.

The servant, knowing that the King would give him a rich reward for such a fine citron, hurried and presented the fruit to him.

"Who gave it to you?" asked the King in astonishment.

"Labdhadatta," replied the servant, and the King knew for the second time that it was not yet time to give riches to the poor man.

Some time passed. Lab continued to serve the King well and the generous Giver of Riches once again thought, "I must try once more." So, once again, he summoned Lab to him, and, for the third time, gave him a citron.

Humbly receiving the gift, Lab thought, "Surely the King is jesting with me! He has given me three citrons now!" Now, as Lab was leaving the palace, he met the Queen, a slender, beautiful woman. Struck by her beauty, he humbly offered her the fruit. She took it to the King, knowing his fondness for citrons.

"Who gave you this?" asked the King.

"Labdhadatta, your attendant," she said.

The King was full of amazement and thought, "Three times have I given Labdhadatta a citron filled with jewels and three times has he given it away, not knowing its precious secret. This proves that Labdhadatta has not yet paid for his sins and cannot yet enjoy good fortune!"

The King had a pet monkey of which he was very fond. The animal, seeing the citron, seized it and ran away with it. The King called for his attendants to bring back the wayward monkey and the citron it had taken.

Lab happened to see the animal on a tree and easily enticed it down. Then he carried the monkey on his shoulder and walked back to the palace. The monkey was still clutching the citron in its hands. Handing the monkey to King Lak, Lab withdrew humbly.

At that moment, the monkey threw the citron to the ground near Lab's feet. It broke open and out spilled the jewels! Lab looked upon the glittering jewels in astonishment.

"They are yours!" exclaimed the King. "This is the

precise moment when your sins have been fully atoned for and you can enjoy riches again!"

Hearing this, Lab fell to his knees in gratitude.

The king was happy that at last the faithful Lab could benefit from his generosity. He not only heaped wealth upon him but also made him a border chieftain, giving him villages, elephants and horses as well as the jewels.

Lab proved to be both capable and loyal. His past evil life completely behind him, he served the great King Lak in happiness and prosperity till the end of his life.

THE STORY
OF ARJUNA

A GREEDY AND EVIL landowner once had a poor woman killed just because of a fruit that she had plucked from a tree in his orchard. This is how it happened.

A thin beggar woman called Prashvati wandered around looking for food. She was going to have a baby, but she had not eaten for several days and it seemed to her that the child inside her was crying for food. She walked through the countryside with her rags beating about her in the cold wind. Finally she stopped in front of a huge mansion with a beautiful well-kept garden.

The mansion belonged to the richest landlord in the region. Near the garden wall grew some mango trees. One of the trees had a branch hanging out over the wall and on the branch hung the juiciest and most luscious mango that Prashvati had ever seen. She longed for the fruit with all her heart, or rather she felt the child inside her wanted it. She took a stick and, after much effort, managed to knock down the mango. Then happily she ate the fruit.

Now the landlord had seen this happen. In great

anger, he sent one of his guards to kill the woman who had dared to steal his mango. Poor Prashvati was beaten to death, but just before she died she gave birth to a baby boy. The strangest thing was that the child was found to be clutching a fruit in his small hands and eating it. The guard was both astonished and alarmed. He thought that this was a sign of misfortune for him for having killed the mother. He took the beggar woman's child home to his wife and together they cared for him. They called him Arjuna.

Arjuna never once loosened his hold on the seed of the strange fruit he had been holding from the time he was born. The years went by and the child grew but he still held the seed tightly in his hand.

One day, when Arjuna was twelve, his adopted mother took him to a forest to gather firewood. There, at last, Arjuna opened his hand and the seed fell to the ground. Instantly it grew into a huge, magnificent tree with a tall, straight trunk and branches that spread outwards providing shade over a great area.

There was no tree in the forest like this tree. Every year the tree produced fruit — but always only one fruit. It was a strange fruit that was seen nowhere else in the land. And every year, young Arjuna nimbly climbed the tree, plucked the fruit and ate it. This he did every year without fail. As he ate the fruit, he became increasingly tall and strong and handsome. Indeed, no young man in the land could match Arjuna in looks and strength   He could perform any feat, and always emerged the winner in wrestling matches with the greatest wrestlers in the country. He could fight any man or beast and win. His fame spread far and wide.

Now, in a nearby land, there was a king called

Manuja who had heard how handsome and strong Arjuna was. He had also heard stories as to how Arjuna preserved his looks and strength, for people were whispering to each other of a strange fruit that gave tremendous powers to this young man.

King Manuja was most anxious to see if the stories were true. He was himself ugly and old with a thin, bent body and wrinkled skin but he was in love with the beautiful Princess Trisala and dearly wished to marry her. However, she was always taunting him about his weakness and ugliness. It was not surprising therefore that King Manuja was most anxious to get hold of the marvellous fruit of which he had heard so much. He wanted to be as young and strong and handsome as Arjuna. So he sent his soldiers to bring Arjuna to the palace before him.

"Is it true that you get your strength and vitality from a magic fruit?" asked the King.

"Yes, it is," answered Arjuna.

The King was now very excited. Ho offered Arjuna a big bag of silver coins in exchange for the fruit. Arjuna refused. The King increased his offer to two bags of silver coins, one bag of gold coins and one bag of pearls. Still Arjuna refused. Nothing that the King said could tempt him to give up his magic fruit.

Angrily, the King ordered his guards to throw Arjuna into prison.

"That would be of no use, sir," said Arjuna. "Nobody but I can pluck the fruit."

Strangely, as the King found, this was so. Only Arjuna could get hold of the fruit; it eluded the grasp of any other person.

The King finally let Arjuna go, but he thought long and deeply on how he could obtain the fruit. An idea

came to him. He ordered his guards to watch Arjuna closely and to wait for the moment when he had plucked the fruit and had it safely in his hands. They were then to take it away from him and give it to the King.

So, one moonlit evening, the guards secretly waited and watched as Arjuna climbed the tree and plucked the fruit. As soon as he came down, they surrounded him, snatched the fruit from his hands and led him back to the palace as a prisoner.

King Manuja was overjoyed when the magic fruit was put on a plate before him. Greedily, he ate it. Instantly he was transformed from an old, ugly man into a young, handsome one! His body was no longer bent so that he stood erect. His wrinkles disappeared and his skin became smooth and supple. Strength and vigour returned to his limbs. King Manuja had never been so happy in his life.

He now went to woo the beautiful princess Trisala. She was most astonished by this change in the King's appearance. However, though she spoke to him in a kinder tone than before, she told him that he was still neither handsome nor strong enough for her. She would marry him only if he were as handsome and strong as Arjuna.

This made the King very angry indeed but he was determined to win the lovely Trisala. He began to wish that the magic tree would yield more than one fruit. If one fruit could do so much for him, he thought, what wonders would several fruit do?

The King sent for the wise man who lived in the hills. He was supposed to know everything, including the secrets of the hills, the mountains and the rivers.

When the King asked him how he could make the tree bear more fruit, he replied, "Your Majesty, the tree will yield more fruit only when the earth is nourished by the blood of a young, strong man."

King Manuja immediately decided to have Arjuna killed and his body buried under the tree. He sent a guard to kill Arjuna. But, as it happened, the guard was persuaded by Arjuna to spare his life in return for a large amount of silver. It was arranged that Arjuna should escape secretly and his place be taken by a leper who had died near the palace gates that

71

morning. Quickly, they carried the leper's body in a sack to the forest where the magic tree was and buried him. The guard then returned to the palace and reported to the King that his mission had been accomplished.

To the great delight of the King, the tree began to bear many fruit instead of just one. They were, moreover, easy to pluck as if they wanted the King to eat them all. And he did. He ate every single one of them.

Did King Manuja grow stronger and more handsome? He would have, if the tree had been fed by the blood of a strong, young man. Instead, it had drawn nourishment from the disease-ridden body of an old leper. As a result, when King Manuja ate the fruit he was suddenly and horribly covered with disease. No doctor in the palace could cure him of it.

The King was so ashamed of his looks that he draped himself in white from head to toe and locked himself in a tower for the rest of his life.

As for Arjuna, he remained strong and handsome for the rest of his life. The tree, after having yielded the fruit that brought disease, stopped bearing fruit for a number of years and then began to produce fruit as before again. And so Arjuna was able to continue to derive strength and power from the magic fruit of the tree that he himself had planted.

THE THREE SUITORS

A BRAHMIN WHOSE NAME was Harisvamin had a daughter who was so beautiful that her beauty was spoken of far and wide. She was named Somaprabha which means "moonlight".

Nobody had ever seen a maiden so lovely, so it was not surprising that when Somaprabha reached marriageable age, many suitors came to ask for her hand. Alas! If Somaprabha was lovely in appearance, she was not in character. She was extremely conceited because of the lavish compliments heaped on her. Her family, consisting of her father, mother and a brother named Devasvamin, made much of her, and treated her as if she were a princess.

Indeed, after a while, Somaprabha came to look upon herself as a princess deserving everybody's attention and service. When she could not get her way, she flew into a violent temper. She became thoroughly spoilt and self-centred, thinking only of her beauty and importance.

She went to her father and said, "Father, I should be given in marriage only to a man who is a brave and handsome hero or to one who possesses vast knowledge or has magic powers. Only such a man will be worthy of me!"

Now Harisvamin loved his daughter very much and wished to please her. He decided to make her wishes known among his acquaintances, so that only those with the desired qualifications would come forward to apply for Somaprabha's hand. He also instructed his wife and son Devasvamin to do the same.

Shortly after this, he was approached by a Brahmin who said, "Sir, I possess magic powers, and therefore you will find me an eligible husband for your beautiful daughter!"

Harisvamin asked him to give proof of his magic powers, upon which the man uttered some words and immediately a fiery chariot appeared from the skies. Harisvamin was delighted and promised to give his daughter to the magician.

At this time, unknown to Harisvamin, his wife was visited by another Brahmin who came to ask for her daughter's hand.

"I am a scholar and possess vast knowledge," he said. "I can see things that others cannot. I have knowledge of the past, present and future!"

Harisvamin's wife asked for proof of this knowledge. To her amazement, he told her of many things in her past which only she knew. She was greatly impressed and promised to give her daughter Somaprabha in marriage to him.

Now a third suitor, unknown to either Harisvamin or his wife, approached Devasvamin and asked for his sister's hand. "I am a hero and I have done many amazing things in the past," he claimed. "I have slain monsters and have crushed the most evil demons in the land!"

He described his exploits in such great detail that Devasvamin was impressed. Besides, he looked so tall and handsome and brave that there could be no doubt that he was a hero. So Devasvamin promised to give him his sister in marriage.

On a certain appointed day, the three suitors came to Harisvamin's house to make arrangements for the wedding. Imagine the alarm of Harisvamin when he found out what had happened! He did not know how to deal with the three suitors.

Then something happened to cause him even greater alarm. His daughter went missing! A thorough search through the house and garden proved to be of no avail. The beautiful Somaprabha had vanished.

"I shall find out where she is," said the suitor who had vast knowledge. "Now let me see." He closed his eyes for he could see things which other people could not with his inner rather than his outer eyes. After a few moments he cried out, "The beautiful Somaprabha has been carried off by the evil demon Rakshasha and is hidden in a cave in the Vindhaya Forest! I can see her clearly! She is a prisoner of the evil one!"

On hearing this, Harisvamin was filled with distress. "Oh, how shall we go to the Vindhaya Forest to rescue her?" he cried. "It's hundreds of miles away!"

"Ah, you leave that to me!" said the suitor who was a magician. "Have you forgotten that I possess magic powers?"

He then uttered some words and lo! A winged chariot appeared from the skies. They all got into it and were soon on the way to the Vindhaya Forest. When they reached the forest, so dark and eerie it was that they were filled with fear.

Soon they heard cries for help coming from a cave. Going towards it, they saw that it was indeed the beautiful Somaprabha who was being kept a prisoner in the cave by the demon Rakshasha. Rakshasha looked most ferocious with his fiery eyes and powerful claws.

"Will no one save me?" cried Somaprabha impatiently.

While the others trembled, the suitor who had called himself a hero came forward.

"Have no fear, I shall rescue you!" he cried. "I have had more terrible monsters to deal with than this Rakshasha!"

With that, he took out his sword and rushed upon the monster. A fierce fight ensued. With a final thrust of his sword, the hero dealt his enemy the death blow. The evil Rakshasha, with a mighty groan, vanished in a burst of heat and light!

The beautiful Somaprabha was safe. But was she grateful? As soon as she was brought out of the cave by the three suitors, she began to complain about having to wait such a long time for rescue to come.

Meanwhile, her father was thinking hard. He was worried. He was wondering which one of the three suitors he should give his daughter to, for all had had a part in her rescue.

"Without my knowledge of where she had been taken to, she would not have been rescued," the suitor with vast knowledge was sure to say.

"Without me, you would never have reached her," the suitor with magic powers was sure to say.

"Without me, the evil Rakshasha would not have been killed," the suitor who was a hero was bound to say.

"Oh, what am I to do?" wondered Harisvamin. He turned to the three suitors and said, "I don't know which one of you deserves to marry my daughter."

"I don't wish to marry her!" said the suitor with vast knowledge.

"Neither do I!" said the magician.

"Nor I!" said the hero.

Imagine the astonishment of Harisvamin and Somaprabha on hearing this! Somaprabha, in particular, was shocked. It was incredible to her that any man would refuse to have her.

"Something happened to make me change my mind," said the suitor with vast knowledge. "When the hero killed the evil demon, there was a great burst of light. This light touched me and made me see that beautiful Somaprabha is not worth having! She may be beautiful but she's bad-tempered, selfish and spoilt. I would not wish to have such a wife!"

"Now, isn't that strange? Exactly the same thing happened to me," said the magician.

"It happened to me too!" exclaimed the hero. "Beauty is worthless unless it is accompanied by virtue. Our eyes have been suddenly opened!"

So the three suitors left, and never returned again. And much as he loved his daughter, Harisvamin had to agree with them. As for Somaprabha, she gradually learnt that virtue is more important than a beautiful appearance.

UDENA

PARANTAPA, KING OF KOSAMBI, an ancient kingdom in India, was overjoyed. At last his queen was going to have a child! For many years, the royal couple had yearned for a child, but they had remained childless. Now, at last, their wish was going to be fulfilled. In his happiness, the King gave his wife a ring with a ruby that was as big as a pigeon's egg.

One night, however, the King had a strange and disturbing dream. In his dream, he saw an old, ugly woman who cried out to him in a shrill voice, "Beware, Parantapa! Beware! You will never see your child! Powerful forces will take him away! Beware! Beware!"

Parantapa woke up feeling very disturbed. He immediately gave orders that his queen was to be guarded at all hours of the day. Her favourite spot was a garden within the palace walls, where she could walk among the peacocks and lotus ponds. The King ordered that taller, stronger walls were to be built around this garden. He wished to make sure that no evil person could come near his beloved queen and the child in her.

One day, the Queen was as usual in her favourite garden. She was feeding the peacocks when a huge, black bird circled in the sky above her. Suddenly it swooped down and carried her off in its enormous claws. The guards and servants around could do nothing to save the

Queen. Tearfully, they then went to report to King Parantapa. He was so enraged that he ordered all of them beheaded. Then he wept.

He was sure that he would never see his wife again and that he would never ever set eyes on his yet unborn child.

What happened to the Queen meanwhile? The huge black bird carried her to the top of a banyan tree and left her there. And there, the Queen gave birth to a baby boy.

Now, living in the same tree was a hermit, a holy man called Allakappa who had once been a king. He looked after the newborn baby, for the poor Queen died soon after he was born. Allakappa called the boy Udena. He fed him with honey which he found in the forests as well as with the sap of certain trees.

Udena grew tall and strong and proved to be a very brave hunter. No boar or tiger could match him in strength. He could run as fast as the wind, and he could send his spears hurtling long distances in the air. The hermit Allakappa looked at Udena and was very pleased.

"Soon it will be time for you to take your rightful place as king," he said.

One day, Udena saw a large black bird circling above him. It was the same bird that had carried his mother many years ago from the palace garden to the top of the banyan tree. The ugly bird came closer and closer, spreading its enormous wings. Udena pulled a huge tree from the ground by its roots and hurled it at the bird. The bird was struck in its heart and dropped down to the ground dead!

Allakappa saw the dead bird and was very pleased.

"It is almost time for you to return, Udena," he said.

Shortly after that, Allakappa pointed something out to Udena. It was a white umbrella and it floated in the sky towards them. Now a white umbrella was a symbol of kingship.

"Udena, it is time now!" cried Allakappa. "I know by this sign that your father is dead, and you must

return to be King of Kosambi before others claim what is yours by right. Get ready now, King Udena."

Then Allakappa brought out a flute with three strings. When he touched the first string, lo and behold, ten thousand elephants appeared! He touched the second string and this time war elephants appeared. Then he touched the third string and a snow-white elephant appeared to take Udena back to Kosambi.

Udena mounted the white elephant and rode in triumph to Kosambi, followed by the other elephants. He wore on his finger the ruby ring which his father had given his mother and which the hermit had kept for him. This was proof that he was the son of Parantapa, King of Kosambi.

King Udena persuaded the hermit Allakappa to live in his palace and become his adviser. He also married a beautiful princess who bore him many sons. Udena was a wise man and he became the most powerful and famous king who ever ruled the kingdom of Kosambi.

THE MAN WITH
ASTOUNDING KNOWLEDGE

THERE WAS ONCE a poor and rather stupid Brahmin named Harisharman. The people in his village often laughed at him for his dullness of mind. His wife and children never complained though, for he was a good husband and father and did his best for them.

Unable to find work in his village, he wandered about with his family and soon came to a city. Here lived a very rich landowner named Sthuladatta who happened to need more servants. Harisharman and his family entered into Sthuladatta's service, doing menial jobs and carrying messages.

One day, one of Sthuladatta's daughters got married, and the rich landowner arranged for a big feast in his house. There were hundreds of guests, including Sthuladatta's relatives. A great deal of food was cooked for the occasion, for Sthuladatta wanted all his guests to have their fill of meat, rice, vegetables and sweetmeats.

Harisharman, his mouth watering at the sight of so much good food, thought, "Somebody's sure to ask me to partake of this food. I can hardly wait for it."

However, nobody seemed to remember him. He became very gloomy and began to complain dolefully to his wife, "It's because I'm so stupid that nobody pays any attention to me! How I wish I could be clever with a great deal of knowledge! Then people would respect me more."

Harisharman then had an idea. He would pretend to be clever and show that he had certain knowledge which no other person had.

One night, when everybody was asleep, he stole out into the stable in which was kept the horse belonging to Sthuladatta's son-in-law. He untethered the horse, a mild creature, and hid it in a wood some distance from the house.

Next morning, the whole family looked for the missing horse but they could not find it anywhere. They were puzzled, and came to the conclusion that a thief had come during the night and stolen the animal. Now, while the search was going on, Harisharman's wife said loudly, as her husband had instructed her, "My husband possesses unusual knowledge. He knows many things that ordinary people do not. Why don't you go to him and ask him where the horse is?"

So Sthuladatta and his son-in-law went to Harisharman and asked him to find the missing horse for them.

Closing his eyes and looking very wise, Harisharman chanted, "Horse, horse, show me where you are!" Then, opening his eyes, he exclaimed excitedly, "The animal is tethered under a large tree in the wood half a mile from this house!"

Sthuladatta sent some servants to the wood. True enough, they found the horse there and brought it back.

How everyone wondered at Harisharman's knowledge! Sthuladatta's wife was very pleased and invited Harisharman to a hearty meal which she herself placed before him.

As Harisharman ate, he felt very happy and satisfied with himself. He was no longer thought of as stupid! People were beginning to respect him.

A few days later, getting bolder, Harisharman secretly took one of the nose-studs that Sthuladatta's wife had carelessly left on a table. He hid it under a bush in the garden.

Finding the nose-stud missing, Sthuladatta's wife was panic-stricken, for it was her favourite piece of jewellery. She ordered the servants to search the house but, of course, the stud could not be found.

Then she remembered the clever, knowledgeable Harisharman. She went to him and asked him to find her nose-stud.

Again, Harisharman closed his eyes and began to chant slowly, "Oh nose-stud, where can you be?" Then he opened his eyes and exclaimed, "It's under a bush in the garden! The bush to the left of the mango tree!"

A search was immediately made and Sthuladatta's wife gave a cry of delight when the nose-stud was put in her hands.

Now everyone was truly amazed at the knowledge shown by Harisharman. They began to tell others about his wonderful ability to see things hidden from others. The stories spread far and wide, until the King himself heard about this remarkable man and was curious to meet him.

An opportunity soon presented itself. The King one day discovered that a certain amount of his gold and

93

jewels was missing. He suspected that one of his servants had stolen the treasure and hidden it. As there were so many servants in the palace, and the palace itself was so large, it would prove extremely difficult for him to find the culprit and recover the treasure. The King decided to send for Harisharman.

When the Brahmin appeared before him, the King said, "I have heard of your astounding knowledge. If you can find my missing gold and jewels, you will get a rich reward! If you can't, you will be punished, for that will mean you have been playing a trick on people and deceiving them!"

Poor Harisharman was secretly distressed. He was sorry he had tricked people into believing that he was a clever man possessed with unusual knowledge.

Alone in his room, he broke into a cold sweat. He began to wail his misfortune and to blame himself for empty boasting. "Oh tongue!" he moaned. "What have you done? You have committed a serious crime! You will certainly be punished."

Now, one of the maidservants in the palace was passing by his room. She heard Harisharman's words and stood still in terror. Her name was Jihva which means "tongue", and she was the one who had stolen the King's treasure and hidden it.

On hearing his words, she thought that the clever Brahmin had found her out, and was now warning her. Rushing into his room, she threw herself at his feet and begged for mercy, crying, "Oh, please, sir, don't let the King punish me! I will tell you where the jewels are! They are buried in a cloth bag at the foot of the pomegranate tree in the back garden."

Harisharman pretended to look very angry. "You are a wicked girl," he said, "and I'm glad I found you

out! I shall tell the King directly!"

"Oh no, sir!" pleaded Jihva. She took a gold coin from her belt and offered it to him, saying, "Please accept this coin, sir, and don't tell the King about me."

Pocketing the coin, Harisharman said severely, "All right! But next time you won't get off so easily!"

Then he went to the King and told him that he had found the hiding place of the treasure. Closing his eyes, he said, "I think I see it in a cloth bag, buried under the pomegranate tree in the back garden!"

The King sent his servants to look, and, true enough, the gold and jewels were found there!

The King was very pleased with Harisharman and invited him to stay in his palace.

"You will be my adviser," said the King. "There'll be plenty of things for you to find out for me, since you are such a clever man."

Harisharman did not dare say no to the King, but in the middle of the night he and his family quietly stole out of the palace and left the city!

"Better to be poor and humble and have peace of mind," thought Harisharman, "than pretend to be clever and suffer agony at the thought of being found out! I have been lucky so far to escape detection. No more such dangerous pretence for me!"

With these thoughts, Harisharman walked on, whistling happily, for there was no more fear in his heart.